RAGGEDY ANN and ANDY
Help Santa Claus

By Polly Curren

Illustrated by June Goldsborough

GOLDEN PRESS

Western Publishing Company, Inc.

Racine, Wisconsin

Raggedy Ann and Andy sat by the fireplace, as quiet as mice. The house was silent and dark.

Everyone else was asleep, but all the dolls were wide-awake and excited. Tonight was Christmas Eve, and the dolls were waiting for Santa Claus!

It was getting late, and Baby Doll was impatient. "Where *is* Santa?" she asked.

"I hope he remembers to come," French Doll worried.

Raggedy Ann held up her hand. "Sh-h-h," she whispered. "Listen. . . ."

They all heard the music of tiny sleigh bells, then a soft thud as something landed on the roof. The next moment—whizzz!—Santa Claus was standing in the living room!

"Ho, ho, ho!" he boomed happily when he saw all the dolls. "Merry Christmas, little friends!"

Raggedy Ann's and Andy's wide smiles grew wider. French Doll curtsied. China Doll bowed low. All the dolls clapped their hands and cried, "Merry Christmas, Santa Claus!"

Raggedy Ann seated Santa in a big easy chair. Andy placed Santa's sack beside him. French Doll served him milk and cookies.

"Just what I need!" Santa declared.

Santa opened his sack and began taking out gifts
and putting them under the tree. Just as he finished
filling the stockings, *bong!* went the clock in the hall.

"Bless my whiskers!" Santa exclaimed. "I must
hurry. I have to go to the Old House this year before
I start home to the North Pole."

The Raggedys and the other dolls were surprised. They thought the Old House had been empty for a long, long time.

"Do children live there, Santa?" Raggedy Ann asked eagerly.

"Ho, ho, ho!" Santa chuckled. "There are three very *good* children—Nancy and Donnie and Paul. I have trains and dolls for them right here in my sack."

Then, quickly, Santa slung his sack up on his back. After placing his finger beside his nose—whizzz!—Santa was gone.

Baby Doll yawned and rubbed her eyes. "I'm sleepy," she sighed.

"As soon as the room is tidy, we'll go to sleep,"
Raggedy Ann said. She started to brush the crumbs
from the floor.

That was when she saw the doll, half-hidden under
the chair. When Raggedy Ann picked up the brand-
new doll, she found a tag that said "To Nancy."

"Oh!" Raggedy Ann cried out. "This little doll must have fallen out of Santa's sack. She belongs to Nancy, down at the Old House."

"We must take her there!" Andy said at once. Then he frowned. "But the Old House is far away. How can we get there?"

Up spoke Fireman Doll. "We can use my fire
engine," he said.

Andy shook his head. "Too dangerous," he said.
"The roads are covered with ice."

"We must find some way," Raggedy Ann said as
she and Andy put their heads together.

At last Raggedy Ann looked up happily. "I know!"
she cried. "We'll use Marcella's sled. We'll ask Fido
and Peterkins to pull it. And Cowboy Doll can use
his rope to lasso the chimney. . . ."

"And you and I will climb up the rope to the
roof!" Andy added, too excited to be quiet any
longer. "We like to climb."

"I'll be the driver," said Fireman Doll.

"I'll lend my blanket," Baby Doll offered.

"I'll bring my rope," Cowboy Doll said.

Raggedy Ann smiled at the brand-new doll. "And I'll hold you very carefully until we get to the Old House," she promised softly. "Santa will leave you there for Nancy."

Off went the dolls to wake Fido and Peterkins, and a few minutes later everything was ready.

"Go!" Fireman Doll called out.

Fido and Peterkins pulled and pulled—but the sled would not move an inch. Raggedy Andy hopped off and pushed with all his might.

Slowly the sled began to move. Just as it started to gather speed, Andy jumped back on.

Faster than a rocket, the sled flew down the long, dark road toward the Old House. The dolls could see Santa on its roof, almost up to the chimney.

"Wait, Santa Claus!" Andy shouted.

"Wait! Wait!" called the other dolls.

Santa looked down and saw the dolls. "Bless my whiskers!" he cried. "What are you doing here?"

Both Raggedys hopped off the sled. Quickly, Cowboy Doll twirled his rope. Then, with one mighty toss, he lassoed the chimney on his very first try.

Andy and Ann climbed up . . . up . . . up the rope, then stepped onto the roof.

"We brought you something!" Raggedy Ann smiled, handing Santa the brand-new doll.

"Nancy's doll!" Santa exclaimed. "Where did you find her?"

Raggedy Ann and Andy told Santa what had happened. "We hoped we'd get here in time to catch you," Ann said.

"And we did!" Andy grinned.

Putting his arms around Raggedy Ann and Andy,
Santa hugged them tightly. And then—Santa Claus
kissed them both! "How can I ever thank you for
your help?" he asked.

"You just did," Raggedy Ann said shyly. Very
gently, she touched the spot on her head where Santa's
kiss had landed.

"You sure did!" Andy added. He, too, rubbed his
"kissing spot."

Back down the rope and to their places on the sled went the Raggedys. All the dolls waved good-bye as Fido and Peterkins headed home.

Santa Claus waved and watched them go. "Merry Christmas, little friends," he called softly. And, turning quickly, he disappeared down the chimney!